The First Forest

Written by John Gile

Illustrated by Tom Heflin

To Renie, my wife, with love,
to our parents with gratitude,
and to our children with hope.

J.G.

To Ashley.

T.H.

The First Forest

Written by John Gile

Illustrated by Tom Heflin

10 9 8 7 6 5 4 3

Text Copyright © 1978, 1989 by John Gile
Illustrations Copyright © 1989 by John Gile

Library of Congress Card Number: 89-91458
ISBN: 0-910941-01-7

Printed in the United States of America
by Worzalla, Stevens Point, Wisconsin

If you wonder in winter when you walk in the snow
Why some trees stand naked while cold north winds blow,

Come with me to visit a woodland I know
Where the first trees were made, long, long ago.

To get there, just place your hands over your eyes
And imagine a tree, any shape, any size:
A muscular monster in leafy disguise

Or a short, chubby shrub with a prickly surprise.
Then imagine another and do it again.
Keep imagining trees just as fast as you can.

Before long you'll arrive, if you follow my plan,
In The First Forest where all tree making began.

The Tree Maker made the first trees with great care
With their roots in the ground and their limbs in the air.
He gave them strong trunks and green clothes to wear
And made certain that all that they needed was there.

He let each tree choose what it would become;
A spruce or a maple, a pine or a plum.
There were hundreds of choices they could pick from
And each choice was sure to be pleasing to some.

The Tree Maker saw that his forest was good
And was pleased as his trees shared their new brotherhood.

He helped each tree learn how to grow as it should
Changing water and sunlight and soil into wood.

Each day in the forest was happy and peaceful
As each day each tree grew more stately and graceful...

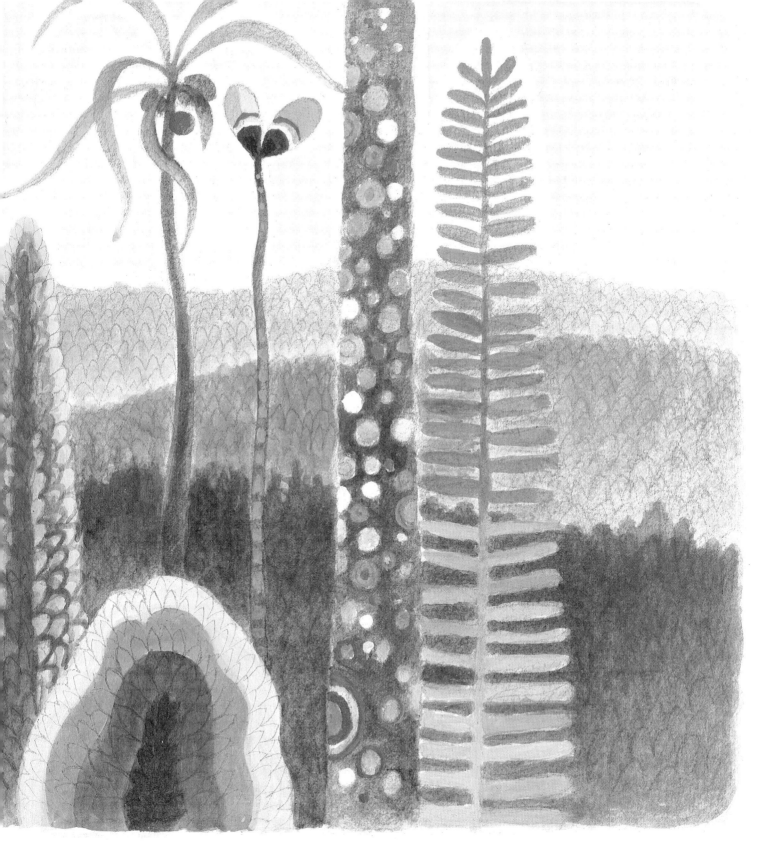

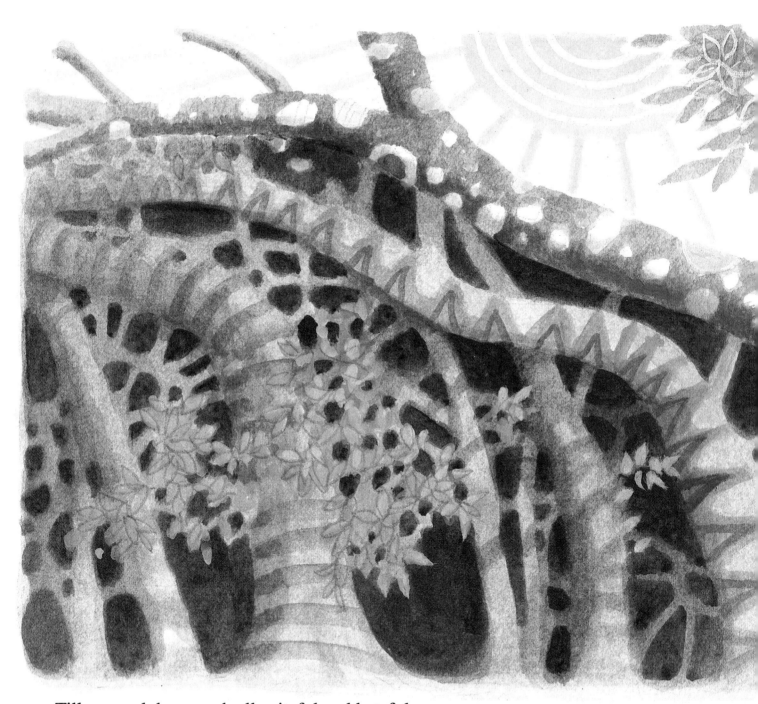

Till one sad day greed, all spiteful and hateful,
Created a scene nothing short of disgraceful.
"If the sun makes me grow," some heard one tree say,
"I'll be biggest and best if I catch every ray."

So he stretched out his limbs and shoved others away . . .
And the peace of the forest was ended that day.

Soon other trees followed that tree's lead like sheep.
They pushed and they shoved, making wounds that went deep.
Broken limbs and dead leaves were knocked off in a heap.

It was so sad it made the willow trees weep.

When the Tree Maker came to his forest that night,
His beautiful trees were an ugly sight:

They were twisted and bare and shaking with fright
Except for a few that stayed out of the fight.

The sight of the mess made the Tree Maker mad.
But the plight of his trees made the Tree Maker sad.
His heart broke in two, he felt so bad,
When he thought of the beauty his trees once had.

Slowly he started to clean up the mess
That had changed his woods into wilderness.
He chased away greed and selfishness
And bound up each wound with tenderness.

Then the Tree Maker did what was hardest of all –
He punished the trees that took part in the brawl.
He ruled that the selfish ones, big and small,
Would lose every leaf from their limbs every fall.

He rewarded the trees that stayed calm and serene
While others were being selfish and mean

With a promise that they would remain ever green
Through summer and winter and seasons between.

That's why in the winter when you walk in the snow
Some trees stand stark naked while cold north winds blow.

But each spring the Tree Maker lets his love show
When he gives back their beauty and makes new leaves grow.

An
Author's
Note on
The First Forest:
Briefly stated, what
I want children and adult
readers to come away with
is a more generous, trusting,
sharing spirit. *The First Forest*
reminds us that greed and
selfishness are harmful and that peace
and harmony flow from an attitude
of grateful appreciation for the gifts
we receive and a respect for the need
and right of others to share in those gifts,
also. The technique is similar to that of Aesop
and others who use fables and allegories to make
a point: readers absorb the lesson as it applies to
their own behavior, not as a characterization
of the animal or element of nature which misbehaves
or acts unwisely. If even one person has a more generous
attitude toward others because he or she is reminded of
The First Forest by a barren tree, an evergreen,
or by a deciduous tree losing leaves in the fall or
growing new ones
in the spring,
we will
have
succeeded.